Miss Happiness
and Miss Flower

Also by Rumer Godden
and published by Macmillan

The Diddakoi
The Story of Holly and Ivy
The Dolls' House
The Fairy Doll

For older readers

The Peacock Spring
The Greengage Summer

RUMER GODDEN

Miss Happiness and Miss Flower

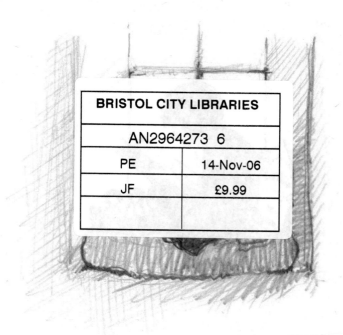

Illustrated by Gary Blythe

MACMILLAN CHILDREN'S BOOKS

First published 1961 by Macmillan

This edition published 2006 by Macmillan Children's Books
a division of Macmillan Publishers Limited
20 New Wharf Road, London N1 9RR
Basingstoke and Oxford
www.panmacmillan.com

Associated companies throughout the world

ISBN-13: 978-1-4050-8856-5
ISBN-10: 1-4050-8856-7

1 3 5 7 9 8 6 4 2

A CIP catalogue record for this book is available from
the British Library.

Typeset by Intype Libra Ltd
Printed and bound in Great Britain by Mackays of Chatham plc, Kent

My thanks are due to Edmund Waller, who designed the Japanese dolls' house described in this book, and who with his brother Geoffrey, aged twelve, made it; to Fiona Fife-Clark, aged eleven, who furnished it, painted the scrolls and lamp-shade and sewed the dolls'-house quilts and cushions; to Miss Anne Ashberry and Miss Creina Glegg, of Miniature Gardens Ltd, Chignal-Smealey, Essex, who made its garden and grew the tiny trees; to Miss Stella Coe (Sogetsu Ryu) for her advice over the meaning of flowers in Japanese lore and for reading the book; and finally and especially to Mr Seo of the Japanese Embassy, for his valuable help and advice and for the loan of books.

Chapter 1

They were two little Japanese dolls, only about five inches high. Their faces and hands were made of white plaster, their bodies of rag, which meant they could bow most beautifully – and Japanese people bow a great deal. Their eyes were slits of black glass and they had delicate plaster noses and red-painted mouths. Their hair was real, black and straight and cut in a fringe. They were exactly alike except that Miss Flower was a little taller and thinner, while

1

Miss Happiness's cheeks were fatter and her red mouth was painted in a smile.

They wore thin cotton kimonos – a kimono is like a dressing-gown with wide-cut sleeves – and they each had a wide sash high up under their arms which was folded over into a heavy pad at the back.

Miss Happiness had a red kimono patterned with chrysanthemums, Miss Flower's was blue with a pattern of cherry blossom; both their sashes were pink and on their feet they had painted white socks and painted sandals with a V-shaped strap across the toes.

They were not new: Miss Flower had a chip out of one ear, her pretty kimono was torn and the paint had come off one of Miss Happiness's shoes. I do not know where they had been all their lives, but when this story begins they had been wrapped in cotton wool and tissue paper, packed in a wooden box and tied with red and white string, wrapped again in brown paper, labelled and stamped and sent all the way from San Francisco in America to England. I do not think they had been asked if they wanted to come – dolls are not asked.

'Where are we now?' asked Miss Flower. 'Is it *another* country?'

'I think it is,' said Miss Happiness.

'It's strange and cold. I can feel it through the box,' said Miss Flower, and she cried, 'No one will understand us or know what we want. Oh, no one will ever understand us again!'

But Miss Happiness was more hopeful and more brave. 'I think they will,' she said.

'How will they?'

'Because there will be some little girl who is clever and kind.'

'Will there be?' asked Miss Flower longingly.

'Yes.'

'Why will there be?'

'Because there always has been,' said Miss Happiness.

All the same, Miss Flower gave a doll shiver, which means she felt as if she shivered though it could not be seen. Miss Flower was always frightened; perhaps the child who made the chip in her ear had been rough. 'I wish we had not come,' said Miss Flower.

Miss Happiness sighed and said, 'We were not asked.'

*

3

Children are not asked either. No one had asked Nona Fell if she wanted to be sent from India to live with her uncle and aunt in England. Everyone had told her she would like it, but 'I don't like it at all,' said Nona.

'Nona is a good name for her,' said her youngest cousin, Belinda. 'All she does is to say No, no, no, all the time.'

With her dark hair and eyes, her thinness, and her skin that was pale and yellow from living so long in the heat, Nona looked a stranger among her pink-cheeked, fair-haired cousins. There were three of them: Anne, who was fourteen, slim and tall; Tom, who was eleven, with freckles; and Belinda, who was a rough tough little girl of seven.

Nona was eight. Her mother had died when she was a baby and she had been brought up by an old Ayah – an Ayah is an Indian nurse – on her father's tea garden, Coimbatore in Southern India. It had been hot in Coimbatore, the sun had shone almost every day; there had been bright flowers and fruit, kind brown people and lots of animals. Here it was winter and Nona was always cold. Her cousins laughed at her clothes; it was no wonder, for they had been chosen by old Ayah who had no idea what English children wore in England, and Nona had a stiff red velvet dress, white socks, black strap shoes and silver bangles. They laughed at the way she spoke English, which was no wonder either, for she talked in a sing-song voice like Ayah.

She did not like the food; living in a hot country does not make one hungry and she had not seen porridge, or puddings, or sausages, or buns before, and 'No thank you,' said Nona. She said 'No thank you' too when anyone asked her to go out for she had never seen so many buses and cars, vans and bicycles; they went so fast it made her dizzy. She said 'No thank you' when her cousins asked her to play; there had been no other English boys and girls in Coimbatore and she had never ridden a bicycle, or roller-skated, or played ping-pong, or rounders, or hide and seek, or even card games like Snap or Beggar-my-neighbour. All she did was to sit and read in a corner or stand by the window and shiver. 'And cry,' said Belinda. 'Cry, baby, cry.'

'Belinda, be kind,' said Nona's aunt, who was Belinda's mother. Nona called her Mother too. 'Be kind. We must all help her to settle down.'

'I don't want her to settle down,' said Belinda.

*

All through Christmas Nona was unhappy and when Christmas was over it was no better. She stood by the window and ran her bangles up and down her wrist, up and down and round and round. They were thin and of Indian silver; she had had them since she was almost a baby and to feel them made her seem closer to Coimbatore.

'Come to the park, Nona. We're going to skate.'

'No thank you.'

'I'm going to the shops, Nona. Come along.'

'No thank you.'

'Have some of this nice hot toast.'

'No thank you.'

At last Mother spoke to her seriously. 'You really must try to be happier, Nona. You're not the only small person to come from far away.'

'I'm the only one here,' said Nona.

At that moment the bell pinged and the postman's rat-tat sounded at the door, and 'You go,' said Mother.

When Nona opened the front door the postman gave her a brown paper parcel. It had American stamps, it felt like a box and was very light. I wonder if you can guess what it was.

*

Nona took the parcel from the postman and brought it to Mother. Written on it was 'The Misses Fell'. 'It's for Anne and Belinda,' said Nona.

'It might be for you as well,' said Mother. 'You are a Miss Fell.'

'Am I?' asked Nona in surprise.

'Don't you know your own name, stupid?' asked Belinda.

Nona shook her head. Ayah used to call her Little Missy, but no one in Coimbatore had called her Miss Fell.

'It's from your Great-Aunt Lucy Dickinson,' said Mother, looking at the writing. 'It must be a late Christmas present.'

'A late Christmas present! A late Christmas present!' shouted Belinda, and she shouted for Anne to come.

'Undo it, Nona,' said Tom.

'Why should Nona . . .?' began Belinda.

'Because I said so,' said Tom in such a terrible voice that Belinda was quiet.

Nona took off the brown paper and found the wooden box with the red and white strings. 'Cut them,' said Belinda impatiently, but Nona's small fingers untied the bow and the knot and carefully smoothed out the strings. 'Oh, you are *slow*!' said Belinda.

'She's not, she's careful,' said Tom.

Nona lifted the lid and carefully, perhaps even more carefully than usual because Tom had praised her, she unrolled the cotton wool and tissue paper, and there on the table, looking very small and cold and white, lay Miss Happiness and Miss Flower.

'What queer little dolls,' said Belinda, disappointed, and Nona answered, 'They're not queer. They're Japanese.'

You can imagine how frightened and lost Miss Happiness and Miss Flower felt when they found themselves on the big slippery table. They had to lie there looking up into the faces of Nona and Belinda. If Nona and Belinda had been Japanese children, one of them, Miss Flower was sure, would have made her and Miss Happiness bow. 'We can't even be polite,' said Miss Flower in despair, and she cried, 'Can one of *these* be the kind and clever girl?'

'Wish that she may be,' said Miss Happiness. 'Wish.' As I have often told you before, wishes are very powerful things, even dolls' wishes, and as

Miss Happiness wished, Nona put out a finger and very gently stroked Miss Flower's hair. Her finger felt the chip, and 'You poor little doll,' said Nona.

'They're not even new,' said Belinda in disgust. 'Stupid old Great-Aunt Lucy Dickinson,' and in a temper she began to crumple up the wrappings. Then she stopped. She had found a piece of paper written on in spidery old-fashioned writing. Mother read it out. It was from Great-Aunt Lucy Dickinson. 'I send you with my love,' wrote Great-Aunt Lucy Dickinson, 'Miss Happiness, Miss Flower and Little Peach.' 'Happiness and Flower,' said Mother. 'What pretty names.'*

'Peach is the one I like best,' said Belinda. 'But where *is* Little Peach?'

'Was there no other doll in the parcel?' asked Anne.

'No. There were only two, not three.'

'Nothing in the wrappings?'

'No.'

'In the cotton wool or tissue paper?'

'Nothing.'

It was very odd. There was no sign of Little

* See note: *Names*, p. 101.

Peach. 'And he is the one I would have liked best,' mourned Belinda.

'Never mind,' said Mother. 'Anne is too big for dolls so there is one each for you and Nona.'

'They have been a long time getting here,' said Anne, looking at the postmark on the brown paper. 'Poor little things, spending Christmas in a parcel.'

'They don't mind about Christmas,' said Nona quickly.

It was strange how Nona seemed to know about these little dolls. '*You* have never been to Japan,' said Belinda rudely.

That was true, but, like Miss Happiness and Miss Flower, Nona had come from far away, and could feel for them. 'Perhaps,' said Miss Flower, 'she might be the kind and clever girl.'

'Why shouldn't they mind about Christmas?' argued Belinda.

'They don't have Christmas in Japan.'

'Don't be silly.'

'I'm not silly. They don't.'

'What do they have then?'

Nona was not sure but, as you know, she was always reading, and it seemed to her that in some story about Japanese children or in a geography book she had read . . . What did I read? thought Nona, wrinkling up her forehead to try and remember. Then, 'They have a Star Festival,' she said.

'A *Star* Festival?'

'Yes,' said Nona. They were all looking at her and she blushed and stammered, though she remembered more clearly now. 'S-something to do with the stars, t-two stars,' she said. 'I think they are the spirits of two people who loved each other long, long ago, a thousand years ago, and were separated. Now they are up in two stars each side of the M-milky Way, and one night each year they can cross and meet.'

'Across the Milky Way?' said Anne. 'How pretty.'

'Yes,' said Nona again, and now her eyes shone so that she, too, looked almost pretty. 'And on earth that night children – grown-up people as well, but mostly children – write wishes on pieces of coloured paper and tie them outside on the bamboos, all over Japan,' she said, her eyes shining.

They looked at her in surprise. 'Why, Nona', said Mother, 'you seem a different child when you tell a story like that.'

'I didn't know you could,' said Anne. 'It's a beautiful story.'

'Jolly clever to remember it like that,' said Tom.

'It comes of reading,' said Father. 'That's what I'm always telling you children. Good girl, Nona.'

He gave Nona a pat on the head and Nona felt so pleased that she smiled at him quite like a happy little girl, but Belinda was not pleased at all.

Belinda was the youngest and she had always been Father's pet, and Tom's and Anne's; she did not like it when they praised Nona. 'You needn't think you're so clever,' she said to Nona when everyone else had gone. 'You can't do anything *but* read . . . and cry, cry-baby. They only say you're clever because you were so stupid before.'

Nona did not answer but the happy look faded from her face.

'Why did you come here?' asked Belinda. The more she talked the angrier she grew. 'Why did you have to come? We don't want you. Why don't you go home? Why don't you have a house and a family of your own?'

Nona still did not answer.

'Star Festival! Rubbish!' shouted Belinda.

'It isn't rubbish,' said Nona in a hard little voice;

12

now she was pale again and her eyes blazed, but Belinda did not see; she had flung out of the room.

When Nona was alone she went and stood by the window and presently a tear splashed down on the window-sill, then another and another. A home and a family of your own . . . 'Coimbatore, old Ayah,' whispered Nona, and the tears came thick and fast.

I do not know how long Nona stood there by the window, but the room, and then the garden, grew dark. She could hear the others talking in the play-room and Mother singing in the kitchen, but she stood there in the dark room staring out of the window.

I wish I could go home, thought Nona. I wish I could see my *own* father. I wish I could see Ayah. I wish . . . Now the wish was so big that it seemed to run out of her right up into the sky, and . . . 'Why, the stars are out!' said Nona.

Across the garden she could see the shapes of trees, bare against the sky, and above them and behind them were stars, bright because of the frosty winter dark. There was a glass door into the garden and Nona opened it and stepped outside. It was so cold that it made her catch her breath, but now she could see the whole night sky. There's the Milky Way, thought Nona – her own father had often showed it to her – and she wondered which of the stars were the two that held the people in love.

By the glass door there was a little tree. It was not a bamboo, of course, but as she looked at it Nona's face suddenly grew determined and she came in and shut the door.

She switched on the light, and taking a piece of paper and a pencil from Mother's desk – 'Without even asking,' said Belinda afterwards – she tore the paper into narrow strips and began to write. 'I wish I could go home,' wrote Nona through more tears. 'I wish I had never come.' 'I wish I was back in Coimbatore.' 'I wish I had a house of my own.' 'I wish there wasn't a Belinda.' She took a piece of cotton from Mother's work-basket, cut it into short bits and threaded one through each of her papers, and rolled them up tightly so that no one could read them. There was a blazer belonging to Tom in the basket, waiting to be mended; Nona slipped it on and went out and tied her wishes on the tree.

It seemed to help her unhappiness to put the wishes on the tree and she went back to write some

14

more, but she had said all there was to say. The Japanese dolls were lying close by her elbow and now she looked down at them. The light caught their eyes so that they shone up at her. I believe *they* like tying wishes on the tree, thought Nona. Of course, it's their Star Festival.

'Our Star Festival!' said Miss Happiness and Miss Flower.

It was not, of course, the right night, but that did not seem to matter. Nona took another piece of paper and cut that up, then ran into the playroom and quietly fetched her paint-box and a cup of water; then she painted the new strips in colours, red and green and blue and yellow. When they were dry she began to write again.

'What is she doing?' whispered Miss Flower.

'Writing wishes.'

'I wish she would write some for us.'

Nona began to cut the strips into smaller, narrower ones.

'What is she doing now?'

'Writing wishes.'

'But such tiny ones. Do you suppose . . .?' asked Miss Flower – she hardly dared say it – 'suppose they are for us?'

'They are for us,' said Miss Happiness, and Miss Flower cried, 'Wishes for the River of Heaven!' which is what Japanese people call the Milky Way.*

Next morning Anne was the first to look out of the window and see the little tree covered with wishes. How pretty they looked with their colours! Nona had found some tinsel left over from Christmas and put that on too, and had cut out some paper flowers. 'Why, Nona!' said Anne, 'how lovely!' Then she looked again and asked, 'Isn't it . . .? Yes, it is. Look,' she called to the others. 'Oh, do come and see. Nona has made a Star Festival all by herself.'

'But not on bamboos,' said Nona. 'You haven't any.'

'But lots of wishes,' said Anne.

'Lots of wishes,' whispered Miss Happiness and Miss Flower. They knew what the wishes were.

'Rolled up like secrets,' said Tom.

'They are secrets,' said Nona quickly. She was beginning to feel ashamed of some of them. 'Secrets,' she said again.

'Secrets!' sighed Miss Happiness and Miss

* See note: *Star Festival*, p. 101.

Flower. They would have liked everyone to read them. 'Because we *do* want to go home,' they said. 'We *do* want a house of our own. We *do* wish Miss Nona could look after us. It's a pity they have to be secrets.' But the wishes were secret no longer; Belinda had slipped out into the garden and was pulling them off the tree. When she had read some she came in and slammed the door.

'How dare you!' shouted Belinda at Nona. 'They're my dolls as much as yours,' and she snatched them up. 'Mother said so,' shouted the furious Belinda.

Two days ago Nona would have let Belinda take the dolls; she would have gone away by herself and read or stood looking out of the window, but she could not bear to see the way Miss Flower hung limply in Belinda's rough little hand. 'Don't! You're hurting them,' she cried.

'They're only dolls,' said Belinda, more angry than ever, and she cried, 'All right. They want a house. They can go in my dolls' house.'

'House? Did she say house?' asked poor squeezed Miss Flower.

'She said house,' said Miss Happiness.

'Like in our wish?' But Miss Happiness was not at all sure this was like their wish.

'How wonderful,' whispered Miss Flower. She would have liked to close her eyes and dream but, of course, dolls with fixed eyes cannot do this.

Belinda knelt down in front of her dolls' house and swung open the door. 'It's a funny kind of house,' said Miss Happiness. For the first time she had a frightened quiver in her voice.

To us it would not have been a funny kind of house, but when a Japanese doll says 'a house' she means something quite different. Belinda's dolls' house was white with gables and a red roof. The front opened, and inside were two rooms downstairs and two rooms upstairs; it had flannel carpets, bits of lace for curtains and was filled full of dolls'-house furniture and dolls'-house dolls all belonging to Belinda.

I am afraid she was a careless child and everything was dusty, dirty and higgledy-piggledy. It looked very higgledy-piggledy to Miss Happiness and Miss Flower. 'I don't want to stay here,' said Miss Flower as Belinda sat her on a dusty chair, on which already there was a large pin. 'Ow!' cried poor Miss Flower.

'I don't want to either,' said Miss Happiness.

Perhaps it was because Nona too had known quite other kinds of houses, and felt so unhappy and strange in England, that she could guess what Miss Happiness and Miss Flower were feeling behind their stiff plaster faces. 'I don't think the dolls' house will do,' said Nona.

'Why not?' said Belinda. She did not see anything wrong. 'I'll make room for them,' she said and she swept the other dolls out of the dolls' house, helter-skelter, bumpetty-bump; the other poor dolls were bumped and bruised, their legs twisted round. 'No! No!' cried the Japanese dolls. 'O Honourable Miss, please no! Oh no, not for us! Oh, the poor dolls! No! No!' Miss Flower remembered how her chip had ached when it was done. She saw a little boy doll with his wig half torn off, a girl doll with a twisted leg, and 'Oh, I can't bear it!' cried Miss Flower and she fell off the chair on to the floor.

'Stupid thing,' said Belinda.

When Belinda said that, Nona grew so angry

and hot that she had to speak. '*She's* not stupid,' she said. '*You* are. Japanese dolls don't sit on chairs.'

'How do you know?'

'I once saw a picture of a Japanese girl serving tea, and she was kneeling on the floor, like this,' said Nona; she took Miss Happiness and made her kneel.*

Miss Happiness had rather more stuffing in her body than Miss Flower; she stayed exactly where Nona had put her and very pretty she looked with her little black head and the big loop of her sash, far more comfortable than Miss Flower had looked on the chair. Then, very gently, Nona took up Miss Flower and straightened her kimono and put her to kneel beside Miss Happiness.

'That's better. That's better,' sighed Miss Flower, and 'Wish, Wish,' Miss Happiness told her. 'Wish that Miss Nona could look after us.'

'Bet they won't like kneeling there for long,' said Belinda. 'The floor's too hard.'

'Cushions,' said Nona. 'Flat sort of cushions.' She said it quite certainly for she seemed to see a heap of bright dolls' house cushions, and she

* See note: *Kneeling*, p. 102.

pleaded, 'Let me try to make them cushions, Belinda.'

Belinda looked at the untidy, dirty dolls' house, then at the two little dolls kneeling on the floor as if they were . . . asking? thought Belinda. Indeed they were. Dolls cannot speak aloud, you know that, but now Miss Happiness and Miss Flower wished: 'Please, Honourable Miss. We are your little nuisances but please let us have the cushions.' It was certainly the first time in her noisy busy life that Belinda had felt a doll's wish, and she was suddenly ashamed, but she was not going to let Nona know that. 'You had better make them a whole Japanese house,' she said mockingly.

'A Japanese dolls' house,' said Anne.

'A Japanese dolls' house?' Nona looked startled. Until that moment she had never thought of such a thing. 'I couldn't. How could I?' asked Nona.

At that moment Miss Flower slipped – you remember she had not as much stuffing as Miss Happiness. She slipped and the slip sounded like a sharp breath and her head sank even lower on the floor. She must have knocked Miss Happiness, for Miss Happiness bent over too, and they looked as if they were very much asking.

'But . . .' said Nona, 'I don't know how.'

'You didn't know how to make a Star Festival, but you made it,' said Tom.

'Not properly,' said Nona, but she was pleased, for Tom was the one in the family who really made things. Anne was clever; she could embroider and paint and sew and weave on her loom but Tom had a proper work-bench in the play-room and was making a model galleon – which is a sailing-ship man-of-war. He was making it most beautifully with endless delicate pieces for masts and spars, decks and rails. Tom really knew, and 'You could make a dolls' house,' said Tom.

Chapter 2

It was a week later. Every day Nona took Miss Happiness and Miss Flower out of their wooden box and dusted them and looked at them. 'But where is our house?' asked Miss Flower every day, and every day they both wished, 'Little Honourable Miss. Oh! please, little Honourable Miss, where is our house?' But Nona could not think how to make a Japanese dolls' house.

She got a big cardboard box and cut out doors and windows, but that did not seem right and the cutting hurt her fingers. She tried to arrange an empty drawer with the wooden box for a bed and some rolled-up handkerchiefs for cushions, but it did not look like anything at all. At last she came to Tom's work-table and stood at his elbow.

He had finished cutting the pieces for the hull of his galleon – the hull is the bottom part of a boat – and now was very busy gluing them together. He knew Nona would not talk as Belinda did and so he did not tell her to go away. She stood quite silently watching his clever careful fingers, and a feeling stirred in her own as if they could be clever and careful too. At last the hull sat up firm and neat between its blocks on the work-table, though the glue was still sticky. Then Nona did speak.

'How did you know how to make it?' she asked very respectfully.

'Learnt,' said Tom, rubbing the glue off his thumbs with a wet rag.

'How did you learn?'

'How did you learn about the Star Festival?'

'Oh!' said Nona. 'You mean . . .' and, as she said that, Tom flipped over the book that had the plan of the galleon in it; it was a paper book filled with

24

patterns and designs, and called *100 Ways to Make a Fretsaw Model*. 'Don't lose my place,' said Tom.

'I didn't know you could learn to *carpenter* out of books.'

'You can learn anything out of books,' said Tom.

'A book like this?'

Tom nodded.

'Oh!' said Nona. She stood by him a moment longer and then said, 'Thank you, Tom.'

Mother was very surprised when Nona appeared in front of her wearing her out-door things, her coat, red cap, boots and gloves. 'Do you want to go *out*?' said Mother.

'Oh, please,' said Nona. She was in such a hurry that the words tumbled out. 'I've got my Christmas money. I want to go to the bookshop.'

'Run along then, dear,' said Mother.

Run along! The excitement faded out of Nona's face. 'By – by myself?' she asked.

'The bookshop is this side of the street. You won't have to cross the road.'

'But . . .' The street with its lorries and cars and bicycles, and all the people, thought Nona; the big boys and the dogs. She shivered.

'If you wait till this afternoon I'll come with you.'

'I can't wait,' said Nona.

As Nona opened the front door all the noise of the street came in: a lorry rumbled past, and a car; a gang of children on roller-skates made a noise like thunder; a big boy whistled. Nona shut the front door and ran upstairs.

She had meant to take off her coat and cap and throw herself on the bed in tears again, but then she caught sight of Miss Happiness and Miss Flower.

They were standing one each side of her clock and . . . Did *I* take them out of the box, thought Nona staring. She must have done, but she had been so excited when she put on her things to go out that she did not remember. Did I take them out of their box? She did not think she had, but there they were, standing by the clock, their feet together, their arms hanging down. It seemed to Nona that they were waiting.

I suppose Japanese people are very brave people, thought Nona, and after a minute she went downstairs and opened the front door again.

*

26

Just as she was going out, Mother called her back. 'Oh, Nona, if you are going to the bookshop be careful to be very polite to old Mr Twilfit. He's inclined to be cross.'

'Cross! He's an absolute old dragon,' said Anne.

'He once nearly bit my head off,' said Tom cheerfully.

Nona began to shake. 'Oh, Anne, come with me.'

'Can't. I'm busy.'

'Tom?'

'I'm busy too.'

Nona turned back to the door.

'He once chased me out of the shop,' said Belinda.

'If I know you, you were touching the books with your dirty hands,' said Tom.

Nona thought, and then went back upstairs and washed her hands. Even paler than usual, but with her head held high, she went out and shut the door behind her.

'She has gone,' whispered Miss Flower.

'And for us,' said Miss Happiness.

'Is it to do with the house, do you think?'

'I think so. We will wait for her to come back.'

Tick, tick, tick went the clock as the minutes

passed. It might have been two little dolls' hearts beating.

Nona's heart was beating too, but . . . once you start being brave you have to go on, thought Nona. She was shaking when she got to the bookshop. Perhaps she expected to meet a real dragon but all she could see in the shop were books, stacks and racks of them, books on shelves and laid on tables, books piled up on the counter. The shop had W. Twilfit, Bookseller, over the window, but though she peeped and peered she could see no sign of anyone at all.

The bell rang as she went in, which made her jump. Very carefully she walked between the tables, and jumped again when she saw a big old man looking at her. In the dark shop he seemed very big, very alarming to Nona; his grey hair stood up in a shock, making him seem even taller than he was, but the most frightening thing about him were his eyebrows that were thick and shaggy as two furred grey caterpillars. When she saw him looking at her, Nona stayed as still as a mouse caught in a trap.

'What do you want? Hey?' His voice was so big that it seemed to rumble round the shop.

'Please' – Nona could hardly make any sound at all – 'Please, have you got a book called *100 Ways to Make a Japanese House*?'

'No such book.' Besides being a rumble it was cross. Nona held on to the edge of a table.

'But Tom said . . .'

'Tom's wrong.'

The shameful tears were near again. Nona bent her head over a book and turned over a page.

'DON'T TOUCH!' shouted Mr Twilfit.

This time Nona jumped so high that she bit her tongue, and the pain and the fright made her speak before she could think. 'I *can* touch,' she said. 'I washed my hands before I came!'

She did not know then that when Mr Twilfit's eyebrows worked up and down, in the way that looked so frightening, it meant that he was pleased. They worked up and down now. '*Washed* them?' said Mr Twilfit, as if he did not believe her.

For answer Nona showed them to him palms upwards. Mr Twilfit bent and looked at them; then he took one, and he could feel how Nona was trembling. 'I didn't know there was a boy or girl in this town,' he said, 'who would wash their hands before they touched books. I beg your pardon, little Missy.'

The rumble was almost soft now. Ayah had called Nona Little Missy. It was too much for Nona; she burst into tears.

'Must it be a Japanese house?' asked Mr Twilfit.

'They are – sniff – Japanese dolls – sniff,' said Nona.

'And you want to make them feel at home,' said Mr Twilfit, and he looked out of the window. Then he said, 'When I was a little boy I knew what it was like to be a long way from home.'

Mr Twilfit had not chased Nona out of his shop, indeed he had taken her into his room behind it and sat her down at his desk while she told him all about Miss Happiness and Miss Flower. His eyebrows worked up and down as she told from the beginning of the postman bringing the parcel, right down to *100 Ways to Make a Japanese House*.

'But I'm afraid I was right,' he said. 'There is no such book. There are others. Can you read?' he rapped out.

'Of course,' said Nona.

'Really read?'

That was one thing Nona was quite sure she could do, and she nodded.

Mr Twilfit got up and went back into the shop; Nona could hear him rummaging and taking down books from the shelves. 'This one is called *Japanese Homes and Gardens*,' he said, bringing in a book. It was nearly half as big as Nona. She took a deep breath.

'I don't think I could pay for one as big as that,' she said.

'It's nearly all pictures. Might be useful,' said Mr Twilfit as if she had not spoken. He went back to the shop. He found another book called *Customs of Old Japan*; then one on how the Japanese arrange flowers, and a book of Japanese fairy tales with more pictures. 'Useful,' said Mr Twilfit.

'I don't understand about the money here,' said Nona. 'Indian money is different.' And she put all her Christmas money, a ten-shilling note, some half-crowns, shillings, sixpences and pennies, on the desk. 'But would this be enough?'

'Can't buy those books,' said Mr Twilfit. 'Out of the question. Cost a lot of money. Will you be careful if I lend them to you?'

31

'Very careful,' said Nona, and her brown eyes glowed.

'Then give me your name and address.'

'Nona Fell,' said Nona dreamily – she was thinking about reading those books – 'Nona Fell. Coimbatore Tea Estate, near Travancore, South India . . .'

'You are in England,' said Mr Twilfit very gently. 'Your address here?'

Nona looked at him and the glow went out of her eyes. She could have fallen through the floor with shame; even small children, almost babies, know their address, but she had been taken into the house almost as if she had been a piece of luggage, and had never bothered to notice or find out its address. 'I don't know,' she had to whisper.

'I see. You weren't interested,' said Mr Twilfit, and Nona nodded with another rush of tears.

'Is it far?' asked Mr Twilfit.

'Just down the road.'

'Come along then,' said Mr Twilfit.

'Good gracious heavens!' said Belinda, who was looking out of one of the front windows. '*Look* at Nona and Mr Twilfit.'

Everyone crowded to the window to see.

'He has a great bundle of books,' said Anne.

'She's bringing him in,' said Belinda.

'Well, I'll be darned!' said Tom.

It was Mother who really brought him in, for it was she who opened the door. 'Nona, I was getting anxious . . .' then she broke off. 'I see you have found a friend.'

'Have I?' asked Nona. She had not thought of having a friend in England, but it seemed like that when Mr Twilfit came in and sat down and had a cup of coffee.

'And we were fetched down to the room to meet the old and honourable gentleman,' said Miss Happiness.

'She made us bow,' said Miss Flower and she sounded just as pleased as Miss Happiness. 'She is beginning to understand.'

Now every day on the playroom window seat three heads could be seen: Nona's dark one, bent, as she sat cross-legged with one of Mr Twilfit's books, and beside her two very small black ones: Miss Happiness and Miss Flower. She had made them two cushions from pieces of old hair ribbon; Miss

Happiness had a red cushion, Miss Flower's was pale blue. 'I like mine best,' said Miss Flower; then she was worried in case Miss Happiness did not like her own, but 'I like mine,' said Miss Happiness.

Nona had no time to stand and look out of the window; she spent all day over Mr Twilfit's books or trotting up the road to see Mr Twilfit. She was learning all she could about Japan; about Japanese houses and gardens and Japanese furniture – though it mostly isn't furniture, thought Nona; about quilts and cushions, bowls and scrolls; about the niche to hold a scroll and flowers; about the way the Japanese arrange flowers. She was learning about Japanese feasts – 'And they do have a Star Festival,' said Nona, 'a New Year Festival and a Feast of Dolls.'

'But not with dolls like us,' said Miss Flower, and she and Miss Happiness said together, '*Honourable* dolls.' Nona learned Japanese names, and about Japanese food and Japanese fairy tales. She was not the only one to learn. 'Everyone else has to learn too,' said Anne, 'willy-nilly,' for Nona sometimes read the books aloud in her sing-song voice. 'Like a reading machine,' said Tom.

'For goodness' sake!' said Belinda, and stuffed her fingers in her ears.

Though Belinda stuffed her fingers in her ears there was one story she always managed to hear. It was in the fairy tale book and was about a boy called Peach. '*We* had a Little Peach who should have been in the parcel but was lost . . . and Mother *still* hasn't written to Great-Aunt Lucy Dickinson,' said Belinda.

The Peach Boy story began with a man and a woman who longed for a child. No child came, until on one hot summer day the woman found a big peach floating in the stream. She took it home for her husband to eat, but no sooner had he touched it with his knife than the top flew off. It opened in two halves and there, in the peach, was a tiny baby boy.

'A *Japanese* baby boy,' said Miss Happiness and Miss Flower.

Belinda loved that story. 'He grew up to be naughty, just like me,' she said, 'and when he was big he went out into the world. I wonder *why* our Little Peach didn't come,' said Belinda.

Chapter 3

Miss Flower could not help being anxious about the house. 'Will Miss Nona know that a Japanese house should have walls that slide open like windows?'

'Paper windows,' said Miss Happiness.

'That it should have a little garden to look at?' said Miss Flower. 'Does she know about quilts, not beds? Chopsticks, not spoons and forks? Cushions, not chairs?'

'You know she knows about cushions,' said Miss Happiness.

'But bowls, not cups?'

'Hush, she is studying.'

Miss Flower tried to hush but she could not help a small whisper. 'It takes so long to study. If we could tell her . . .'

'We can't.'

'What can we do for Honourable Miss?'

'We can wish,' said Miss Happiness, and they wished. Perhaps Belinda felt the wishing more than Nona, for, 'Is she going on reading for *ever*?' asked Belinda.

It really seemed as if Nona would go on reading for ever, but one snowy afternoon Mr Twilfit knocked at the door. He had brought a book. 'Not *another* book!' said Belinda.

'Hush, Belinda,' and Mother asked Mr Twilfit to come into the drawing-room where they all were; but Belinda would not hush.

'She has read and read,' said Belinda, 'and she *still* doesn't know how to make a Japanese house.'

'I do know,' said Nona, and they all looked at her.

'Well, how?'

37

'I don't exactly know how but I know what it should be like.'

'Well?'

Miss Happiness and Miss Flower, who had been brought down on their cushions, held their breaths.

'Japanese houses are up off the ground,' began Nona, 'so the house should stand on stilts – or up on a box, I thought, with little wooden steps. Some of the walls should be plain, but the other walls should slide like windows; they should be rather like picture frames but with plain paper criss-crossed with wood. Some of the inside walls should slide too, but they are plain.'

'Yes,' breathed Miss Happiness and Miss Flower.

'The roof should be tiles, dark blue or grey . . .'

'Yes. Yes.'

'Inside, there should be a little hall for taking off shoes. Japanese people don't wear shoes in the house. The rooms should be almost empty, with matting on the floor, if we could get it fine enough,' said Nona. 'Lots of homes nowadays do have chairs and sofas and beds but most still have cushions to sit on, and they would have cupboards with sliding doors, or else chests, where they keep rolled-up quilts or mats for beds.'

'Yes,' said Miss Happiness and Miss Flower.

'They would have a firebox – I don't know exactly yet what that is – and in the room there should always be a niche, an alcove for a scroll – that's a Japanese picture – and, by it, a vase of flowers, very few flowers,' said Nona.

'Yes. Yes,' cried Miss Happiness and Miss Flower, and 'Bravo!' said Mr Twilfit.

'Nothing else?' asked Belinda. 'No tables or chairs?'

'A very little table just off the floor.'

'It will look very bare.'

'Japanese houses *are* bare.'

'That is their beauty,' said Mr Twilfit, and his eyebrows worked up and down as he looked at Nona. 'You'll see,' said Mr Twilfit. 'It will be all right once you have got the bones.'

'Do houses have bones?' Nona and Belinda asked him together.

'The foundations, the floors, walls and roofs are the bones. How will you get those, hey?' asked Mr Twilfit.

'They could be carpentered,' said Nona.

'You can't carpenter,' said Belinda.

'No, but . . .'

'But?' Once again they all looked at Nona.

'Tom can,' said Nona with a rush.

'I don't make girls' things,' said Tom.

'Of course they *are* more difficult and delicate,' said Mr Twilfit, and he asked Mother, 'Was it Sir Winston Churchill or the President of the United States who made that beautiful dolls' house for his sister?'

'I don't believe they did,' growled Tom under his breath.

'And of course,' said Mr Twilfit – his eyebrows were busy – 'you would need to be a really good carpenter.'

'I'm making a model galleon,' said Tom.

'And that's horribly difficult,' said loyal Belinda, but Mr Twilfit shook his head.

'That's a model from a plan,' he said, 'Quite, quite simple, you only have to follow it. A Japanese dolls' house wouldn't have a plan. I don't suppose anyone has made one – not in this country. The plan would have to come out of your own head. A boy could hardly be expected to do that.'

'I don't see why not,' said Tom, but Mr Twilfit still shook his head.

'How would you raise it?'

'Make a plinth,' said Tom. 'Like a box upside down,' he explained quickly to Belinda before she could ask him what a plinth was.

'Then the grooves for the sliding walls, they would have to be so very small . . .'

'I could make them,' growled Tom.

'And the frames to hold the paper screens. For a dolls' house they would have to be so very thin. How could you join them?'

'I could,' growled Tom.

But Mr Twilfit still shook his head. 'It would be very difficult,' and, as he stood up to go, he said to Nona, 'You had better save up and we'll see if we can find a proper carpenter.'

Tom scowled at Mr Twilfit – a scowl is a face you make when you dislike someone – and spoke across him to Nona. 'I'll make it for you,' said Tom and under his breath he said to Mr Twilfit, 'You'll see.'

'Nona, would this box be big enough?'

'Nona, if I make this two feet long . . .'

'Would this paper be thick enough for the screens?'

'Nona, I found this shell . . .'

A strange thing had happened. Suddenly it was as if everyone in the house were helping to make the Japanese dolls' house. 'Everyone except me,' said Belinda. 'I won't help.'

Perhaps it was Nona's reading aloud, or Mr Twilfit's interest, or the plan that Tom had drawn from the pictures in the books, 'or because of our wishing,' said Miss Happiness and Miss Flower, but all the family seemed to be running backwards and forwards to Nona, asking Nona questions, bringing things to Nona. 'Except me,' said Belinda and kicked the table.

'Belinda, you're not jealous of Nona?'

'Of course I'm not jealous,' said Belinda scornfully. 'I'm not even interested in Japanese dolls.' That was not quite true; she very often thought about Little Peach. He would have been like Peach Boy in the story, thought Belinda. To think about him took away the feeling Belinda was beginning to have, a feeling of being left out. 'I *wish* Little Peach had come,' said Belinda.

Chapter 4

'Have you chosen the site?' asked Father. ('You see, even Father is joining in,' said Belinda.)

'What is a site?'

'The plot or place where you build.'

'I'll build it on my work-table,' said Tom.

'But it can't stay there,' said Nona.

'No jolly fear,' said Tom.

'Besides, it has to have a garden.'

'If it has a garden, it should be near a window. Plants need light and air,' said Mother.

'Plants?' Until that moment Nona had not thought of a garden with real plants. 'Where should we find them?' she asked.

'In the fields and woods.'

'Could we take them?'

'Of course. They're wild.'

In Coimbatore flowers grew on trees or creepers or else in the gardens. 'You mean little flowers growing around *loose*?' said Nona amazed. She seemed to see a dolls'-house-size garden full of flowers of dolls'-house size. 'Could we make it on my window-sill?' she asked. 'Could that be the site?'

'Well, I had thought of an old table . . .' said Mother.

'*Please.*'

'Oh, let her, Mother.'

'Very well.'

It seemed to Belinda that everyone was spoiling Nona. Belinda kicked the door as she went out.

At the cabinet-makers' Tom found a piece of rosewood. It was dirty and chipped, 'but it's real rosewood,' said Tom, and when he had sand-papered it smooth it was a deep, soft rose-brown colour. 'It will do for the top of the plinth,' said Tom. 'I shall make it a base.'

'But what next?' asked Miss Flower; she still could not help feeling anxious.

Next was a visit to the wood shop. 'A wood shop?' asked Nona. She had never heard of one.

'You can buy pieces of wood, all lengths and sizes, narrow bits and wide ones. I hope you have some money,' said Tom.

Nona had the ten-shilling note, the half-crowns, shillings, sixpences and pennies she had shown to Mr Twilfit. She had her ninepence a week pocket money saved up as well. 'Will that be enough?' she asked Tom.

'Come and see.'

'Come? How?' Tom was getting his bicycle out. 'You mean on the back? With my legs hanging down?' said Nona in horror.

'Of course not. That isn't allowed,' said Tom. 'I'll ride very slowly and you can run beside me.'

'*Run?* In the street? I couldn't,' said Nona.

'O.K. No wood,' said Tom. 'I'll get on with my galleon.'

The rosewood floor stood on Nona's window-sill; Miss Happiness and Miss Flower stood near it.

'Bicycles go so fast,' said Nona.

Miss Happiness and Miss Flower appeared not to hear.

'Tom whizzes in and out, between buses and cars.' They still seemed not to hear.

'Japanese people are *horribly* brave,' said Nona.

They did not contradict her, and Nona came and stood by Tom's table. 'O.K., I'll come,' she said.

The wood shop was a most wonderful place. There were big blocks and planks of wood, tiny delicate mouldings, thin strips, narrow bits and wide ones; there were chair legs and stool tops, every kind of corner and grooving, and handles from great front door ones down to the smallest dolls'-house size. There were sheets of wood of every kind, stains and paints, screws and hinges.

What did Tom buy? 'A terrific great lot of wood,' Nona told the others when she got home. She thought it wonderful that Tom knew what to ask for and that the shopman knew what he meant. 'Because *I* didn't,' said Nona.

It was all packed up and Tom tied the long bits of wood to the cross-bar of his bicycle; the screws and nails and pots of stain and glue and paint he put in his pockets. 'But you'll have to carry the rest,' he told Nona.

'*And* run?' asked Nona faintly.

Tom looked at her. 'Belinda would,' he said.

'O.K.,' said Nona and picked up the parcel.

When you build a real house there is the sound of bricks being piled, of the concrete mixer, of wood being sawn and hammered, of lorries and shouts. The sound of a dolls' house being made is different; there is a tap, tap, tap from a little hammer, the shirring of sandpaper, the whirring noise of the fine drill as Tom made his drill holes; but the building noises made by Tom meant as much to Miss Happiness and Miss Flower as the sound of your real house being built could mean to you. Nona had taken them and their cushions into the playroom so that they could see.

'What is he doing now?' whispered Miss Flower.

'He is making the corners.'

'And now?'

'He is making the hall.'

'And now?' asked Miss Flower.

'He is making the two side walls.' And then one day Miss Happiness cried, 'Oh, Flower . . .'

'Yes?'

'He is making . . . a niche.'

'A niche? For our scroll and flowers? Oh, Happiness!'

Tom and Nona had argued about that niche. 'But I *told* you,' said Nona. 'It's a most important part of a Japanese room.'

'Be darned if you did,' said Tom.

'But I *did*. A niche like a little alcove. I did.'

It took Tom four days to think out how to make that niche, but at last he found a way. It was fitted into one of the side walls, making a small alcove in it. 'We'll make it a separate little roof,' said Tom, 'and a low floor inside.'

'Oh, Tom, you are clever,' said Nona.

'Honourable, clever Mr Tom,' said Miss Happiness and Miss Flower.

Tom planned to make an entrance hall. He divided the front of the house into one big window and a small hall. 'A shoes-off place,' said Miss Happiness.

'It should have sliding screens inside *and* out,' said Nona.

'Christopher Columbus!' said Tom. He might

well have said it, for they were small and finicking to make, but he made them.

The windows were made of frames, latticed like the sliding screens, on hinges that Tom took off two old cigar boxes of Father's. They swung back so that Nona could open the front of the doll's-house when she wanted to play.

Now the front of the house was finished, and the side walls and the niche were painted, and fixed against the end pillars. Soon, from pillar to pillar, Tom would fix the heavier beams that would hold the roof.

'But what about the screens?' asked Nona. 'The sliding screen doors in the back wall and for the hall?'

'I'll make them,' said Tom. He sounded tired.

'But when? When?'

'Christopher Columbus!' said Tom. 'Can't I ever have a day off?'

To make the sliding screens was most difficult of all. 'I need six hands,' he said. At last he had put in the two back screens with their paper lattice and the plain and latticed screens for the hall; and it was a wonderful moment when Tom and Nona could slide them all backwards and forwards, backwards and forwards. 'Let Mr Twilfit see *that*!' said Tom.

Now the walls were up, and the house only needed the roof 'to have all its bones,' said Nona, remembering what Mr Twilfit had said; but before the roof could be made, something happened that Nona had forgotten about. The something was school.

'I can't go,' said Nona.

'Anne goes, Tom goes, Belinda goes. Of course you must go.'

'No thank you,' said Nona, but it was no use saying 'No thank you', as this was one of the times children were not asked; and one morning Nona had to take off her red velvet dress, her white socks and silver bangles, and dress herself in a tunic and blouse like Anne's and Belinda's, a dark blue coat and a cap with a badge. Then, carrying a case that held a new pencil-box, a ruler and her money for lunch, she walked with Anne and Belinda to school.

She came home in tears. 'I knew she would,' said Belinda. 'She cried all day.'

'You mustn't cry here,' the teacher, Miss Lane, had told Nona.

'It's here I want to cry,' said Nona, and she did. Belinda was ashamed, but Belinda did not know how terrifying the big strange new building seemed to Nona. There seemed to be hundreds of girls and so much noise and bustle that it made her head swim. They, too, laughed at the way she spoke, and the little girl she sat next to, a pretty little girl with long golden curls, would not speak to her. By the time they reached home Nona was sick with crying and Belinda was so angry her cheeks were bright red.

Mother led Nona to the fire and took off her coat and cap and gloves. She gave her some hot tea and brown bread and butter; Belinda had some too, and by and by they both felt better.

When they had finished, Mother took out her sewing. The fire was warm, the sound of the needle going in and out was quiet and calm. Nona felt tired but she did not cry any more. She sat on the rug and leant against Mother's knee.

'You'll have to go again tomorrow,' said Belinda.

Then Mother said, 'Why not take Miss Happiness and Miss Flower to school?'

'They wouldn't be allowed,' said Belinda at once.

'How could I take them?' asked Nona. 'In my pocket?'

'No, in your head,' said Mother, and before they could argue she said, 'If you took them in your pocket that would be breaking the rules, and you mustn't do that, but you could take them in your head.'

'How?' but a watery smile came on Nona's face.

'You say Japanese pictures are scrolls, with painting and writing?'

Nona nodded.

'In school you can learn how to write beautifully and to paint.'

'Can I?'

'You read to us that in Japanese houses they have matting on the floors. You could learn to weave mats on a loom.'

'Like Anne?'

'Certainly. Anne learned to weave at school. Then you can learn to sew. There are all those quilts and cushions to make and the dolls need new kimonos. Miss Lane teaches you to sew nicely. Even Belinda is learning to make tiny careful stitches.'

'I'm not,' said Belinda.

*

'Do you hear the honourable lady?' whispered Miss Flower.

'Kimonos, quilts, cushions,' said Miss Happiness, her eyes shining.

'Tiny careful stitches!' and together they both sent a fresh wish to Nona: 'O Honourable little Miss Nona, please go to school. Oh, go to school!' And Nona began to think that perhaps school might not be so very dreadful, particularly as Tom said, 'I'll work for you every Saturday until the house is finished.'

It took a long time. 'Saturday after Saturday,' grumbled Tom. Half-term came and went and still the house was not done. 'Children are so slow!' groaned Miss Flower.

That was the first and only time Miss Happiness got cross. 'Slow? They are wonderfully quick,' she cried. 'Quick and kind and clever. Don't you ever let me hear you say things like that again,' cried Miss Happiness, and her little glass eyes flashed.

'We must do the roof,' said Tom one Saturday, and he said, 'In a real house when that is done a bough is put in the chimney and the builders are given beer.'

'Do you like beer?' asked Nona.

'Ginger beer,' said Tom.

'When the roof is made,' said Nona, 'I'll buy you a bottle of ginger beer.' But how was the roof to be made?

'It should be tiles,' said Tom. He had drawn tiles in the plan, tiles like little scallops in rows; now he had to think how he could make them.

There was an old tea chest in the garage. It was stamped in big black letters. Tom looked at it. 'It's the right thickness,' he said. He took it to pieces and from two of the sides he cut panels and glued them into place against a ridgepole.

Nona looked at the great black letters. 'But . . .' she began in dismay.

'But what?' asked Tom, as if he could not see anything wrong.

'It looks *horrid*!' said Nona. 'Not a bit like tiles. And why have you put the lettering outside?'

'Why not?' asked Tom.

'It shows.'

'It won't show,' said Tom.

'But it does,' said Nona, almost tearfully.

'Wait and see,' said Tom.

He sounded as if he knew exactly what he was doing, but Miss Flower could not help being anxious too. 'Will it be all right?' she whispered to Miss Happiness. 'Will it?'

'I think it will,' said Miss Happiness.

'Are you sure?'

'Mr Tom has made the house beautifully. He will make a beautiful roof as well. We should trust Mr Tom,' said Miss Happiness.

Miss Flower wanted to trust Tom but she thought it wise to do some wishing as well. 'I wish the house could have a pretty roof. I don't see how it can but I wish it could,' she wished.

'How much money have you got?' Tom asked Nona.

She had four shillings, and Tom went with her to the bookshop, where they bought a large sheet of stiff drawing-paper. Then they bought a pot of dark blue poster paint. Mr Twilfit did up the paper in a roll. 'It's for the dolls' house,' Nona told him.

'It's getting on, hey?' asked Mr Twilfit.

'Very well, thank you,' said Tom coldly, and Mr Twilfit's eyebrows went up and down as he watched Tom walk away out of the shop.

When they got home Tom stretched the paper on his work-table and he and Nona painted it evenly, a deep blue. In the afternoon when it was dry he sat Nona down at the playroom table and told her to cut the paper into long strips, two inches wide. 'Measure carefully,' and he said cheerfully, 'You can manage it.'

Nona looked at the beautiful paper and was not at all sure she could manage it. 'W-won't you do it, Tom?' she asked.

'You must do *some* of the work,' said Tom severely. 'I have to bike down to the wood shop. I need a piece of wood.' He took some more money from Nona and went off.

Nona sat and looked at the paper – she was very afraid she would spoil it. Very carefully she measured off two inches at each side, making dots to mark the width . . . But how can I keep the cutting straight? thought Nona. Still very carefully, with the big scissors, she started to cut across from dot to dot and, sure enough, the strip was uneven and wandered up and down.

'Silly billy! You'll never do it like that.' Anne had come quietly into the playroom to practise.

'Then *how*?' asked Nona desperately, looking at

the dreadful jagged strip she had made. 'Oh, Tom will be so cross,' and she looked as if she were going to cry.

'Look. Fold it,' said Anne, putting down her music.

'Oh, Anne, please help me.'

'You must measure,' said Anne.

'But I *did*. Two inches.'

'Right,' said Anne. 'But you need a knife, not scissors.' She took a knife from Tom's work-table and cut off the uneven piece Nona had left, then measured two inches again, marking with dots as Nona had done, folded the paper, and then slit along the fold; a smooth two-inch strip came off. 'Now try,' said Anne.

'Oh, Anne. You do it.'

'I haven't time.'

'P-please, Anne. I don't want to make Tom cross.'

'Well, I'll fold it. Then you try,' said Anne. 'Come on. It's easy.'

It was easy – 'when you know how,' said Nona. With Anne folding the paper and holding it steady, Nona was able to cut off an even strip.

'And strip after strip,' said Miss Happiness in pride.

'Anne, you have such very clever, neat hands,' Nona was saying.

'So have you, Miss Nona,' said Miss Flower.

When Tom came back the strips were laid out on his table, even and smoothly cut, and he was pleased. 'But now we have to scallop them,' he said. 'Anne, you're the neatest one. You do them.' He did not beg Anne, he ordered her. 'I wish I were a boy,' thought Nona.

'What about my piano practice?' Anne said it as if she would far rather make the scallops.

'Practise afterwards,' said Tom. 'Get the scissors, Nona.'

'They're here,' said Nona, hoping Tom would not look in the wastepaper basket and see the strip she had spoiled.

Anne folded each strip four times and with the scissors cut one edge into even scallops. As soon as they were cut, Nona unfolded the strip and, with a deeper blue pencil, Tom marked a line between each scallop: scallop after scallop, strip after strip. It took longer to mark the lines than to cut the scallops, and when Anne went to the piano to practise, Tom, with Nona to wait on him, was still at work.

After tea Anne helped again. Nona brushed the back of the strips with glue, making them really sticky, and Anne and Tom stuck them one at a time on to the roof panels; they began at the bottom and glued them each a little above the first so that the scallops overlapped. As one row of scallops rose above the other, they began to look very like tiles, and when the roof was covered bottom to top, back and front, Nona and Anne clapped.

'I told you we could trust Mr Tom,' said Miss Happiness.

As Anne and Tom started to make a tiny tiled roof for the niche, Nona slipped out and all by herself went to the grocer. She had to cross the road but, holding her purse very tightly, she crossed it. She was not nearly as afraid now as she had been that first day when she set out for Mr Twilfit's shop. At the grocer's she spent two of her last three ninepences on two bottles of ginger beer; the grocer gave her coloured straws for nothing. On her way home, as she was not sure Anne liked ginger beer, she stopped at a flower barrow and bought a spray of white blossom; she had no money to buy any more.

Miss Happiness and Miss Flower were puzzled

when they saw Nona arranging the ginger beer on a tray. 'We should have served tea,' said Miss Flower, and she said longingly, 'In the tea ceremony.' 'Ceremony' is a word Japanese dolls use a lot; it means doing something in a very respectful and special way.

'In England it is the ginger beer ceremony,' said Miss Happiness, and she comforted Miss Flower. 'See, our Miss Nona knows how to arrange flowers almost as we do; she does not put too many in the vase.' Miss Happiness did not know that there had been only one ninepence left.

'And plum blossom means hope,' said Miss Flower.

'It *is* hope,' said Miss Happiness. 'Look, Flower, look!'

Nona had put the dolls on the pretty tray she was carrying to the playroom. She had stopped just inside the door, looking. Now Miss Flower looked too, and 'Aaah!' whispered Miss Flower.

On Tom's work-bench stood the little house with its tiled roof, its tiny hall and the screen walls that slid, its two side walls and the niche. There was, of course, no chimney, but where the chimney might have been Tom had put a twig of green leaves for a bough.

'How happy and gay they all are!' said Miss Happiness.

'One person isn't happy,' said Miss Flower, and suddenly she had a doll shiver. 'Listen,' said Miss Flower.

'Belinda, have some ginger beer.'

'I'm busy.'

'Belinda, come and see the Japanese house with its new roof.'

'I'm very busy.'

Belinda was still feeling left out. The next time she went into the playroom she gave Tom's work-table a good shake, but Tom had made the house so well that nothing moved or broke. 'I wish Japan were at the bottom of the sea!' said Belinda; but it was not Japan that made her miserable, for as soon as she heard the story of Peach Boy again or thought about Little Peach she felt warm and comfortable; it was when she thought about the Japanese dolls' house – 'and Nona!' said Belinda, gritting her teeth – she felt so jealous and cold and hard that she might have been a small iron Belinda.

Chapter 5

Nona was still not very happy about going to school. 'Why, Nona?' asked Mother. 'Belinda doesn't mind and she is younger than you.'

'It's all right for Belinda,' said Nona. 'She has lots of friends.'

'You can have friends.'

'No I can't,' said Nona tearfully.

'Why not?'

The tears overflowed. 'There's only one girl I like and she sits next to me,' sobbed Nona.

'If you like her why should you mind?' asked Mother, mystified, which means she could not understand at all; it certainly was difficult to understand. 'Why should you mind?' asked Mother.

'She's too pretty and stuck-up to speak to me.'

'She means Melly,' said Belinda. 'Melanie Ashton. You know, her mother keeps the hat shop.'

'But Melly's a nice little girl.'

'She won't speak to me.'

'Perhaps she's shy.'

'No, I'm the one who's shy,' wept Nona.

Except for Melly, school was not really so dreadful now. Nona was learning to write and paint and sew, as Mother had said. When she read aloud now it was not in a sing-song, and nobody laughed at her English. Then one day, on the new page of her reading book, she came across a tiny poem. It was so small it might have been made for a dolls' house:

> My two plum trees are
> So gracious . . .
> See, they flower
> One now, one later.

Underneath was written: 'Haiku. Japanese poem.'*

'Are all Japanese poems as little as that?' Nona asked Miss Lane. 'Are they all as little?'

'Not all, but a great many,' said Miss Lane.

'Could I copy it?' asked Nona, and began to tell Miss Lane about Miss Happiness and Miss Flower.

'Is the house finished?' asked Miss Happiness.

'Oh no!' cried Miss Flower, and 'Now I have to make the steps,' said Tom.

The steps were four pieces of wood, the same length but different widths. Glued one on top of the other, they made a set of steps leading up to the front door. 'You can put dolls'-house tubs of flowers each side,' said Tom.

'Is the house finished now?' asked Miss Happiness. No, it was not finished yet.

Tom stained the frames and the angle pieces a beautiful dark brown. He had painted the walls and the underside of the roof an ivory colour, but the niche he painted pale jade green. Last of all the house was dusted and cleaned, carried into Nona's

* See note: *Haiku*, p. 102.

64

room from the playroom, and put on the window-sill. 'Now show that to Mr Twilfit!' said Tom.

'First it must be furnished,' said Nona. 'I need scraps of cotton and silk.'

'You haven't got any,' said Belinda.

That was only too true. The pieces in Mother's scrap-bag were bits of flannel and oddments from old cotton dresses. There was some velveteen, but velveteen is thick and heavy for a small doll. 'I need thin bright silk in different colours,' said Nona.

'Well, you can't have it.'

'I know I can't,' said Nona mournfully. She had spent that week's ninepence on extra things for Tom. 'And I need a lamp and a low table, and the book says Japanese people keep their quilts in cupboards with sliding doors. How can I . . .' Nona broke off and sat quite still. 'A cupboard with slid-ing doors,' she whispered.

'Nona, I'm talking to you,' said Mother. 'I'm ask-ing you if you want any more pudding?' These days Nona often had more pudding, but now she did not answer.

'Nona. Are you dreaming?' Yes, Nona was dreaming – of Melly's pencil-box.

It was a new pencil-box of plain light wood. It had a compartment down the middle and, most fascinating of all, it had a roll top of slatted wood that rolled back as soon as you touched it. 'It would make a perfect little cupboard,' dreamed Nona, 'empty and standing on its side. Perfect!' And then a daring thought came to her: I wonder if Melly would swap it? – Nona had not been in school very long but already she knew all about swapping. Swap, but for what? It would have to be something very beautiful. After lunch Nona went slowly upstairs and pulled out her drawer; next morning when she went to school she wore her silver bangles.

'Oh, how pretty!' said Melly.

Nona had seen Melly looking at the bangles and had pulled the cuff of her blouse back so that they would show more as she let her hand lie on the desk. They clinked gently against one another and their silver shone above the wood of the desk. 'You like them?' whispered Nona.

Melly nodded, and her curls bobbed. Nona slid off the bangles and when Miss Lane was busy she passed them to Melly. '*Very* pretty,' whispered Melly, looking at them.

'You can put them on if you like.'

Now that they had spoken Nona could not think why she and Melly had not spoken before.

Perhaps Mother had been right and Melly was shy; she blushed as she slid the bangles on. They looked beautiful on her pink and white wrist, and 'Very, *very* pretty,' whispered Melly.

Nona felt an ache in her heart; she had had her bangles almost since she was a baby and they reminded her of Coimbatore, but she had the dolls to think of now. 'I'll swap them if you like,' said Nona.

Melly's grey eyes widened. 'But . . . they're silver!' she said.

'Yes, but I'll swap them.'

'For what?'

'For your pencil-box,' said Nona lightly, but her heart was beating.

'Melly Ashton, Nona Fell, are you talking?' asked Miss Lane, but the two heads, Nona's dark one and Melly's with its golden curls, were bent over their desks, and their pens scratched away. Yet, if Miss Lane had noticed, she would have seen that Melly's pencil-box was on Nona's desk and Nona's bangles were on Melly.

*

Standing on its side in the Japanese doll's-house the pencil-box did look like a real cupboard. 'The quilts shall go in the bottom – when I have the quilts,' said Nona. 'The bowls in the top – when I have the bowls.' The rolltop slid backwards and forwards like a real cupboard.

'It might have come from Japan,' said Miss Flower, and Miss Happiness said, 'It has "Made in Japan" stamped on it. I saw it.'

'Nona, you are to go into the drawing-room. Mother wants you,' said Anne.

'You have done something,' said Belinda. 'Mrs Ashton is there.'

'Who is Mrs Ashton?' asked Nona.

'Melly's mother,' said Anne.

'What have you done?' asked Belinda.

Mrs Ashton was sitting on a chair by the fire when Nona came in. In her hand she held the bangles.

'They're quite valuable,' she was saying to Mother. 'Real silver. I'm sure you wouldn't want Nona to give them away and I couldn't possibly let Melly accept them.'

'But I didn't give them,' said Nona. 'I swapped them.'

'Swapped them?'

'For Melly's pencil box.'

'A *pencil box*?' Both the mothers stared at Nona as if she were ill.

'But you could buy a pencil box for a shilling or two, you silly child.'

'Not that one,' cried poor Nona. 'There isn't another one like that. Oh, don't you see? That's the only one that will do.'

Mrs Ashton was very like Melly, with the same golden hair and grey eyes, the same smile. Nona had spoken to Melly, and now she found courage again. 'If you would come upstairs,' she said, 'I could show you,' and she slipped her hand into Mrs Ashton's. It was the first time Nona had put her hand into anyone's since she had left Coimbatore.

Mrs Ashton looked at Mother, who nodded. 'Show me,' said Mrs Ashton.

'But Mother will make you give it back,' said Belinda. 'You needn't think she won't.' And sure enough, 'You must give it back,' said Mother.

'But Mrs Ashton wasn't cross,' said Nona.

69

'All the more reason,' said Mother.

'And Melly didn't mind.'

'But you are not allowed to swap things at school, not expensive things,' said Mother. 'I'm sorry, Nona, but you must keep the rules.'

Very slowly Nona took the pencil box out of the house.

'It is right and proper,' said Miss Happiness with a sigh. 'She must keep the rules.'

Miss Flower did not answer. She was too sad.

Indeed it seemed that the dolls' house was not getting on at all. On the way to school Nona and Belinda passed a shop where, in the window, four dolls'-house tea sets in delicate flowered china were set out. 'What about those?' asked Belinda.

'It's bowls, not cups, I need,' said Nona.

'There's a sugar bowl.'

'Only one.' Each set had two cups, a teapot, a milk jug and a sugar bowl.

'You could knock the handles off the cups,' said Belinda cheerfully.

'And give them something chipped!' said Nona. She knew without being told that Miss Flower would not like that. 'Anyway, they are four shillings and sixpence each,' she said.

Another shop had table mats in fine, fine bamboo. 'Like dolls'-house matting,' said Nona, 'and Japanese houses always have matting on the floor.' But the mats were a shilling each, 'and I should need two,' said Nona. In the same shop as the tea sets was a round dolls'-house table in dark wood. 'If Tom cut the legs shorter it would look Japanese. Oh, I don't know where to begin!' said Nona, and pressed her face against the glass of one shop, then another. In the end she bought the table, and Tom, with his smallest saw, cut the legs down for her so that the table was only an inch from the floor. It was just right for a Japanese table, but it looked bleak and plain in the empty room. 'It will *never* be furnished,' said Nona.

Miss Flower was terribly alarmed. 'You heard what she said,' cried Miss Flower, and if she could have wrung her little plaster hands she would. 'Never be furnished! Oh, we're only dolls. What can we do?'

'Wish,' said Miss Happiness. She was still smiling. Perhaps that was because her smile was painted on her face, but it made Miss Flower angry.

71

'What's the good of wishing?'

'You never know,' said Miss Happiness.

You never know. Sometimes when things seem farthest off they are quite near. Next morning Melly came to school with a small bundle. She put it on Nona's desk. 'Mother sent you this,' she said.

The bundle was wrapped in a piece of soft paper. Inside were scraps and pieces and snippets of silk, satin and taffeta, in pink and scarlet, blue and lemon colour, white, green, purple and mauve.

'But . . . but . . . how did she *get* them?' asked Nona.

'Well, she does make hats,' said Melly, and laughed at Nona's face. 'These are bits left over. And she says if your mother will let you come to tea she, my mother, will help you with the cushions and quilts. She's a very good sewer,' said Melly.

Nona hardly knew if she were standing on her head or her heels. To go to tea with Melly; to make the quilts and cushions; to have this heap of soft and beautiful stuffs! 'What *is* the matter with Nona?' asked Father, who happened to be looking out of the window as Nona and Belinda came back from school. 'She looks as if she were dancing on the pavement.'

Then, at the beginning of the holidays, it was Easter.

Nona had not kept Easter before. She had never seen Easter eggs or Easter rabbits or chickens. 'Your own father has sent me some money from Coimbatore,' said Mother, 'to buy you all Easter eggs. Ten shillings for each of the others,' she told Nona, 'a pound for you.'

'A *pound*!' said Belinda, her eyes round.

'Is that twenty shillings?' asked Nona. She was trying to do a sum in her head.

'You could buy an enormous huge great Easter egg for that,' said Belinda. 'One of those huge chocolate ones with chocolate and chickens inside.'

'Oh no!' cried Nona.

'No?'

'Please, please no,' – in her agitation Nona could hardly speak – 'I don't want an Easter egg.'

'Not want an egg for *Easter*?'

'No. At least, only a tiny one, about sixpence.'

'Well, what is it you want?'

'Four tea sets,' said Nona, 'and two table mats.'

'What extraordinary things to want.'

'I want them,' said Nona certainly.

*

On Easter Sunday, as they were coming back from church, Melly came up the road to the gate. She was carrying a package tied with yellow ribbon. 'Why, Nona! She has brought you another Easter egg!' but it was a queer shape for an Easter egg, for the package was long and thin. Before Nona opened it she knew what it was, and her fingers began to tremble. 'It's your pencil box.'

'Not mine,' said Melly. 'It's the same as mine. Mother bought it in London in the same shop. Happy Easter,' said Melly, and ran off.

Happy Easter!

'In Japan we have the New Year Festival,' said Miss Flower, 'when fathers and mothers dress the children in their best clothes and take them to visit the shrines and give them money.'

'Lots of money,' said Miss Happiness.

'That is something like this,' said Miss Flower.

'But I like Easter,' said Miss Happiness, and she said, 'We have the Star Festival, of course, and the Boys' Festival, when the boys have paper carp fish and play games.'

'But I like Easter,' said Miss Flower, and she said, 'We have the Doll Festival, when the festival dolls are brought out and the little girls put them up on steps covered with red cloth.'

'I think this is a doll festival day,' said Miss Happiness, smiling.

Indeed, it seemed to be, for the Japanese dolls' house was almost finished at last. The pencil box stood against the wall; the quilts were rolled up on its bottom shelf. Nona had been to tea with Melly on two or three Wednesday afternoons when the hat shop was shut, and after tea they had sewed quilts and pillows, pale pink for Miss Flower, while Miss Happiness had blue.

On the Tuesday after Easter, Nona had hurried over breakfast and run all the way to the shops in case the tea sets were sold, but they were still in the window and she had been able to buy all four.

'*Four* tea sets?' Belinda had asked.

'So that I can get four bowls.'

'And waste all the cups?'

'I have to,' said Nona sadly.

'Christopher Columbus!' said Belinda, just like Tom.

Nona put the cups, the jugs and all but one teapot on one side, but the four sugar bowls and all the plates and saucers and the one teapot she arranged on the top shelf of the pencil box; with its green leaves and pink flowers the china looked Japanese.

Japanese people eat their food with polished sticks called chopsticks: Nona cut pine needles into inch lengths to make some, and they were put beside the china. From the table mat shop she chose two mats in fine cream-coloured bamboo; they almost covered the floor when they were put down. On the matting were cushions made from Mrs Ashton's bright silks; Nona set them round the low table.

'It must be ready now,' said Belinda, but Nona shook her head.

Tom helped to make a lamp from an empty cotton reel.* He ran a flex up through it with a tiny electric bulb and Nona made a paper shade to fit it. She cut a strip of stiff paper, painted it deep pink and joined it into a circle with sticky-tape. 'And I'm going to model a lantern in clay, like the Japanese stone lanterns, for the garden,' she said.

'What garden?' asked Belinda.

'The garden I am going to make.'

Every Japanese house has a firebox.† Nona made hers from a matchbox, painted dark brown and

* See note: *The Lamp*, p. 104.
† See note: *The Firebox*, p. 104.

76

filled with shining red paper from a Christmas cracker. Tom put another of his tiny bulbs in it and joined the flex to the lamp. When it was lit the firebox seemed to glow.

'Now we need a scroll,' said Nona, 'and I must put flowers in the niche.'

'Well, put some,' said Belinda, but Nona said, 'I have to learn about them first.'

'Learn about flowers? Pooh! What is there to learn? Oh Nona, you are so slow.'

'*Please* leave Honourable Miss Nona *alone*,' wished Miss Happiness and Miss Flower. 'Leave her. She is doing things in the Japanese way.'*

Flowers, in Japan, can have meanings: pine branches are for strength; plum blossom means new hope; irises are used for ceremony; while the peony is the King of Flowers.

'Irises and peonies are too big for a dolls' house,' said Anne.

Of course they were too big, but now, in April and May, as Mother and Anne had told Nona, there were wild flowers everywhere in the grass and along the hedges and in the fields and woods just

* See note *Flower Arranging*, p. 104.

outside the town. Nona had never seen anything as lovely and every day she discovered something else; wild violets did for irises and wood sorrel or anemones made white peonies, while eyebright looked like doll's-house lilies. In front of the Japanese dolls' house she made a path of sand and bordered it with cowries, tiny shells she had brought from Coimbatore. At the foot of the steps she put two little china-blue egg-cups, the kind that are like tubs, and filled them with lady's-slipper. Then she begged a big old meat tin from Mother and put it on the window-sill beside the house; she covered it with a layer of earth and moss. Following the pictures of Japanese gardens in Mr Twilfit's big book, she arranged a path with flat stones, and a little heap of pebbles to hold the shell that Anne had given her. The shell was filled with water and made a pool, and by it Nona planted some tufts of grass to look like bamboos, and tiny flowers to look like bushes. 'Japanese gardens have to look natural, like hills and lakes and streams,' she said, and she made a stream of bits of broken looking-glass set in the moss, and by it she set the clay lantern she had modelled. Miss Lane had let her fire it in the school kiln and it had a gloss on it like stone. It looked like a toadstool with a hole in the hood. When a bit of birthday cake candle was put in, it shone over the garden at night, 'and it's quite safe,' said Nona. 'The clay won't catch on fire.' The garden was beautiful, 'but I do wish I had some trees,' said Nona.

'There aren't trees as small as that,' said Belinda.

There was no scroll yet, but in the niche Nona put a vase of flowers. For the vase she used her ivory thimble, and for flowers she chose a scarlet pimpernel – 'That's a peony, the King of Flowers' – and with it were stalks of grass – 'Dolls'-house bamboo,' said Nona. 'Bamboo means luck.'

'Yes. Yes!' breathed Miss Flower.

It was finished. 'They can move in tomorrow,' said Nona.

'Tomorrow!' Miss Happiness felt as if all of her were warmed by the firebox, but Miss Flower felt as if she might crack. 'I shan't close my eyes all night,' she said. They could not close in any case, but she meant that she would not sleep.

'Our house!' said Miss Happiness. 'Tomorrow we move into our house.'

'Yes!' Then Miss Flower stopped. 'We haven't

moved in yet. Suppose . . . suppose something were to happen and prevent . . .'

'But what could?' asked Miss Happiness.

Miss Flower did not know, but all at once she felt cold.

'Can I have a feast?' Nona was asking.

'You can ask some people to tea,' said Mother.

'Can I ask Mr Twilfit and Miss Lane and Mrs Ashton and Melly? And you and Father and Anne and Tom – and Belinda of course?'

'I'm not coming,' said Belinda.

'Why should Nona have people to tea?' asked Belinda, and kicked the corner of the table leg. 'It's not her birthday.'

'Now, Belinda . . .'

Belinda kicked the corner of the table leg again.

'If you do that,' said Mother, 'you can go upstairs at once.' Then she put her hand on Belinda's shoulder and said gently, 'Belinda. Nona has worked so hard. Don't spoil it'; but Belinda shook Mother's hand off, kicked the table leg harder than ever, and ran upstairs.

It was no wonder that Miss Flower trembled.

Chapter 6

The dolls were to have a feast too. 'A tea party,' said Nona.

'A tea ceremony,' said Miss Flower.

Belinda's dolls'-house food was a cardboard ham glued on a plate, some plaster fish glued on another and a plaster pink and white cake. 'That won't do at all,' said Nona, and she went to see Mr Twilfit to find out about a Japanese feast. In the end a beautiful little feast was set out on the low table: a bowl of rice made of snipped-up white thread –

nothing else was fine enough; a saucer of bamboo shoots made of finely chopped grass; a saucer of pink and white sugar cakes made from crumbs of meringue cut round; and some paint-water tea. '*Green* tea?' asked Belinda.

'Japanese people drink green tea.'

'Huh! You know everything,' said Belinda, who was in a very bad temper. 'Everything!' she said. 'But there's one thing you don't know.'

'What is that?'

'Wait and see,' said Belinda, and she looked angry and pleased at the same time.

The dolls were dressed in new kimonos; Father had given Nona an empty cigar box and she kept their clothes in that. Mrs Ashton had made Miss Happiness a white kimono embroidered with a tiny pattern of leaves, over an under-dress of pale yellow silk, and with a sash of blue. Miss Flower's was coral pink over an under-dress of delicate violet colour, and her sash was pale green. Their hair was brushed and their socks and sandals had been painted. Tom had carefully patched the chip on Miss Flower's ear with some white paint and repainted Miss Happiness's shoe. 'We look quite new,' said Miss Happiness.

'Is it really going to happen?' asked Miss Flower. Even though she was dressed she could not quite believe it.

'It really is,' said Miss Happiness.

In the dolls' house the house lamp and the fire-box were switched on, and the lantern was lit. In the real house the front door bell rang, and 'It really is,' said Miss Flower.

Everyone brought presents. Melly had a packet of water flowers, the Japanese paper flowers that uncurl into brightly coloured patterns when you drop them into water. 'You can put one or two in the shell for water lilies,' said Melly.

Mrs Ashton brought a tiny paper sunshade she had once found in a cracker. 'It's from Japan,' she said.

'Quite right,' said Miss Happiness and Miss Flower.

Miss Lane had brought her present in a match-box; it was a length of paper three inches long and an inch and a quarter wide – if you measure with your ruler you will see how big it was. Top and bottom it was held on two matchsticks that Miss Lane had sandpapered smooth and fine; the paper could roll up on them, and on the paper, in fine, fine painting, was some white plum blossom and a bird; the bird was no bigger than a pea. There was some writing too, but so small that to read it you almost needed a magnifying glass, and Nona cried, 'It's my poem!'

> My two plum trees are
> So gracious
> See, they flower
> One now, one later.

'Who could have done it?' asked Belinda.

'It looks like a fairy but I think it was Miss Lane,' said Nona.

'A scroll! A right size Japanese scroll!' said Miss Happiness.

'But shouldn't the writing have been Japanese?' asked Miss Flower doubtfully.

'Not in England. That wouldn't have been polite,' said Miss Happiness, and Miss Flower was satisfied.

Nona hung the scroll in the niche. 'Soon I must make you a new one,' said Miss Lane. 'This one is for spring but you should change them with the seasons.' Miss Happiness and Miss Flower gave two doll's nods, which means they nodded though you could not see them, and said, 'Quite right.'

Anne had made two pleated fans, no bigger than your finger nail. 'It says they should wear fans for the tea ceremony,' said Anne.

'Very right,' and Miss Happiness and Miss Flower were glad when the fans were tucked into their sashes.

Tom had made two tiny pairs of wooden clogs of the kind Japanese ladies use to walk in in the mud, fastened with a loop of scarlet cotton. 'O Honourable Tom!' said the dolls.

All the presents were beautiful but the best of all was Mr Twilfit's. He had brought two trees. 'Are those *trees*?' asked Belinda. 'Real *trees*?'

'A pine and a willow,' said Nona looking at the labels. She sounded dizzy, as indeed she was, for how many people have heard of or seen a pine tree ten inches high and a willow only seven? 'But – they're real, alive!' cried Nona.

'Quite real,' said Mr Twilfit, his eyebrows going up and down.

'I didn't know,' said Miss Flower with great respect, 'that there was anything like that in England.'

'England is indeed a most honourable country,' said Miss Happiness.

'They are grown for people who make sink gardens,' said Mr Twilfit. 'Dwarf gardens in sinks or basins.' Everyone was so enchanted that he was beginning to feel shy and his eyebrows grew still. 'Better plant 'em,' said Mr Twilfit abruptly, and he turned away to look at the house. As he looked he forgot to be shy and his eyebrows began to go up and down again. 'The President couldn't have made it any better,' he said to Tom.

The best of a dolls'-house garden is that it takes only five minutes to plant a tree. Nona planted the pine by the shell, the willow by the stream. They made the garden look exactly like the gardens in the book.

Then Nona turned to the dolls. She made them bow to the company – which means all the people there – and said, 'Miss Happiness and Miss Flower, will you come into your home?' but before they could be made to walk up the path bordered with shells and past the tubs of lady's-slipper, Belinda spoke:

'Not Miss Flower,' said Belinda. 'She's mine.'

*

'Belinda! Belinda! You're not going to spoil it?'

'Yes I am,' said Belinda.

Mother had taken Belinda to the playroom to talk to her. Belinda stood hard and angry by the table; her cheeks were red and her eyes very blue and bright. She argued with Mother.

'On the parcel it said "The *Misses* Fell". You said Anne was too old for dolls and we could have one each. You *said* so,' argued Belinda.

'But that was long ago,' said Mother.

'Miss Flower's mine,' said Belinda. 'You can't take her away from me.'

'It's just that you don't want Nona to have her,' said Mother sadly. 'Oh, Belinda! Belinda!'

'I don't care,' said Belinda.

'That's true,' said Mother. 'You never cared or thought about Miss Flower or wanted her.'

'I want her now,' said Belinda, and she took Miss Flower and threw her into her own dolls' house and slammed the door.

Belinda ate her tea very quickly. Her cheeks were still red, her eyes an even brighter blue. She talked a great deal and said funny things to make everyone laugh, but it was an odd thing that nobody laughed at them except Belinda. No one else really talked and nobody ate very much. Nona ate nothing at all and her face looked white and sick with disappointment; Belinda saw Melly steal a hand into hers, and 'Can I have another meringue?' asked Belinda; and when she put it into her mouth she laughed and blew the sugar crumbs all over the table.

'I think we will go into the drawing-room,' said Mother. 'Belinda, you had better finish your tea alone.'

In the dolls' house the lantern threw a soft light into the house where the front was open and the screens had been slid back to show the garden; the lantern made a reflection in the looking-glass stream and gave the tiny trees real shadows.

Miss Happiness knelt on her cushion in front of the table set ready for the tea ceremony, but she did not touch any of the tea; opposite her was the blue cushion, empty, and a little empty bowl.

'Oh, why couldn't Miss Belinda have taken me?' mourned Miss Happiness. That would have been dreadful enough, but she was stuffed fuller than Miss Flower and her plaster had not been chipped.

'Miss Flower wanted the house even more than I did,' mourned Miss Happiness. 'She was always frightened.' If dolls could have tears I am sure they would have rolled down Miss Happiness's plaster cheeks. 'Oh, I'm afraid!' cried Miss Happiness. 'I'm afraid that Miss Flower will not be able to bear it. I'm afraid she will break.'

There was certainly not a sound or movement in Belinda's dolls' house; not the smallest doll rustle.

When tea was over the guests quietly went home. 'Shan't we play any games?' asked Belinda, astonished.

'We would rather not play with you,' said Anne.

'Because you're a little rotter,' said Tom.

Belinda put out her tongue at him, which was not at all pretty for it still had crumbs of meringue sticking to it.

'You had better go upstairs,' said Mother.

Nona put out the lantern, and switched off the lamp and the firebox. She washed the bowls and platters and put them away. Then she unrolled the blue quilts – the pink ones stayed in the pencil box cupboard – and gently she laid Miss Happiness down and covered her up. Miss Happiness looked very small and lonely in the big room and when Nona slid the paper screens shut they made a s-s-s-sh like a sigh.

Belinda sang and danced all the time she was going to bed; it was odd then that the house should have felt so silent. Tom and Anne had gone to their rooms to do their homework; usually they did it with friendly calls from room to room, but now they shut their doors. Nona had got into bed without a word and lay with her face turned to the wall. Downstairs in the drawing-room Father and Mother talked in low tones. 'What a fuss about a doll,' said Belinda.

No one answered. She half thought of going to the dolls' house and taking Miss Flower out and throwing her at Nona, but 'I'll be darned if I will,' said Belinda.

Saying 'be darned' like Tom made her feel very big and important and she shouted and gargled as she did her teeth.

The house still stayed quite silent.

*

Belinda always went to sleep as soon as her head touched the pillow; only once, long ago, when she had had a cold, she had woken up in the night with a sore throat and stuffy nose. She had not got a cold now but there seemed to be something the matter.

She tossed and turned and twisted. She heard Anne and Tom go to bed, and then later – hours and hours, thought Belinda – Mother and Father came up.

'I can't go to slee-ep,' called Belinda. It did not sound loud, it sounded like a bleat, but Mother did not come in or give Belinda a glass of hot milk as she had that other night. Mother went into her room and shut the door.

Belinda was so surprised that she got out of bed and padded in her bare feet to Mother's door and knocked. Mother opened it a crack. 'I can't go to slee-ep,' wailed Belinda.

'I'm not surprised,' said Mother and shut the door.

Then Belinda felt something queer in her eyes and in her chest, as if something hot and aching were gathering and coming up. Quietly she went back to bed and burrowed under the clothes, but up the aching came until it spilled over; it was wet and splashed down on her pillow. It was tears.

'It's no good crying.' How often Belinda had said that to Nona, but sometimes it is good. As the tears soaked into Belinda's pillow the hard angry feeling seemed to melt away, and 'I'm sorry,' sobbed Belinda, 'sorry.' But she did not cry herself to sleep, she cried herself awake, perhaps more awake than she had ever been in her life.

It is lonely for a little girl to lie awake in the dark when everyone is sleeping, and then Belinda remembered she was not the only one who was alone.

Miss Happiness was alone in the Japanese dolls' house, and what of Miss Flower? Miss Flower was worse than alone in Belinda's dolls' house. Belinda had thrown her in and slammed the door. I threw her quite hard, thought Belinda. Did she break? And suddenly Belinda was more miserable than ever, so miserable that she could not stay in bed any longer; she had to see what had happened to Miss Flower. 'What did I do to Miss Flower?' asked Belinda, and more tears ran down her face. She got out of bed and tiptoed into the playroom.

When the dolls'-house door banged shut on Miss Flower I think she fainted. That was just as well, for when Belinda found her she was lying on her back with one foot in the air, her head under a broken chair and her hand in the dolls'-house wastepaper basket in which there was an earwig. Her kimono and hair were covered with dust, and the chip had opened again under the white paint into a trickle of plaster, but Miss Flower knew nothing until she felt a gentle hand come in and lift her. It was so gentle that she thought it was Nona's; she never dreamed it could be Belinda.

Very gently Belinda lifted Miss Flower, put her leg straight, dusted her hair and clothes and shook the earwig off on to the carpet. Then she stood holding Miss Flower in her hand and wondering what to do next. Suddenly she tiptoed into Nona's room, where the Japanese dolls' house was shut and dark on the window-sill.

As Belinda slid the screen walls back they did not make a s-s-sh like a sigh, but a s-s-sh as if there were a secret – as indeed there was; for carefully, with two fingers, Belinda opened the pencil box cupboard and took out the pink quilts; carefully she unrolled them – and how clumsy her fingers were, though she tried to be careful. She unrolled the quilts beside Miss Happiness, and carefully put Miss Flower in and covered her. Then she slid the screens shut and tiptoed back to bed.

She was quite comfortable now and she went to sleep at once.

Chapter 7

It was a very strange thing. When Belinda had gone to bed nobody had seemed to like her. Now in the morning everybody liked her very much.

Nona came running into her room. She looked a new Nona now with her eyes shining and her hair flying, her cheeks pink. She jumped on Belinda's bed and in a moment they were hugging one another. 'I never thought we would do that!' said Belinda.

Mother came and gave her a kiss. Father ruffled

her hair on his way to the bathroom and at break-
fast everyone seemed to take her part.

'I had Miss Happiness *and* Miss Flower. It wasn't
fair,' said Nona.

'We should have seen Belinda wasn't left out,'
said Anne.

'I'll make you a Japanese dolls' house if you
like,' said Tom, but as the days went on Belinda did
not really want a Japanese dolls' house, though she
liked playing now and then with Nona's. 'But I
wish there were something for me,' said Belinda.

It was summer now. They all wore thin clothes and
sun hats, went bathing and ate ice cream. The shops
were full of cherries, then of peaches; perhaps it
was the peaches that gave Nona her idea.

Miss Happiness and Miss Flower spent much
of their time in the garden and took it in turns
to carry the paper sunshade. Nona put clover
for chrysanthemums in the flower vase in the niche
– chrysanthemums are Japan's own flowers – and
planted them in the egg-cups by the steps. The tiny
willow tree blossomed.

Miss Happiness and Miss Flower had summer
kimonos of pale blue, and Anne wove them two

flat hats of yellow straw. Mr Twilfit, Mrs Ashton and Melly often came to visit them. Miss Lane sent a scroll for summer, with a lotus flower and a butterfly. In the evenings the garden lantern shone pale in the dusk. 'How beautiful it is,' said Miss Happiness, and Miss Flower had a moment of being frightened; her chip had been painted over again but she still could not forget the night in the dusty dolls' house. 'Miss Nona has opened our travelling box again. Why? Why?' she asked; but Nona was only studying the piece of paper that said 'I send you Miss Happiness, Miss Flower and Little Peach.'

'Mother, did you ever write to Great-Aunt Lucy Dickinson?' asked Nona.

'Why! I forgot!' said Mother.

'Could a letter get to America fast?' asked Nona.

'Of course it could, by air.'

'If I write to Great-Aunt Lucy Dickinson, will you help me to buy the stamp? It's a secret,' said Nona.

The stamp cost one shilling and threepence, nearly two whole ninepences. This is the letter Nona sent:

'Dear Great-Aunt Lucy Dickinson,

Miss Happiness and Miss Flower are well. We have made them a new house, but where is Little Peach? He wasn't in the box. Please send him.

From your loving niece, Nona Fell.

P.S. When you answer please put "Privit".'

That was how she spelt 'private'; as you know, she had not been at school very long. She wanted the answer marked 'private' so that no one else would open it. Then she added something else:

'P.P.S. Please send him quickly.'

After Nona had posted the letter she began to look in the shops to see how big the peaches were.

It was three weeks later, a hot sunny morning, and they all had peaches for breakfast.

'Christopher Columbus!' said Tom. 'Is it some-one's birthday?'

'Yes,' said Mother, and Nona giggled.

Miss Happiness and Miss Flower were at break-fast too. They had paint-water tea on their table, tomatoes which were berries and white cotton rice;

they ate with new pine needle chopsticks. There were fresh trefoil flowers in the vase – trefoil looks like dolls'-house yellow chrysanthemums – and everything was extra fresh and tidy. '*Is* it a birthday?' asked Tom.

Miss Happiness and Miss Flower had their heads bent over their rice, but their glass eyes looked as if they were twinkling.

The biggest peach was Belinda's. It was so big that it looked as if it were spilling over her plate. 'Hey, I ought to have that one!' said Father.

'It's Belinda's,' said Mother, and Nona gave another giggle.

Mother showed Belinda how to slip her knife in to slit it, but as Belinda touched it, the peach seemed to wobble, then came in half. Belinda's eyes grew rounder and rounder; for there, in the middle of the peach, was a boy doll baby.

'A *Japanese* boy doll baby,' said Miss Happiness and Miss Flower.

He was little and fat, perhaps two inches high, wearing nothing at all, but with black hair – there was a piece of paper over it to protect it from the peach juice but Belinda snatched it off. His eyes were black glass slits and he had a smile just like Miss Happiness.

Belinda stared and stared. Then, 'How?' she cried. 'How?'

'Never mind how,' said Mother, and Nona said, 'Who is it?'

With her eyes like bright blue saucers Belinda whispered, 'It's . . . It's Little Peach.'

Notes

Names. The names of Japanese girls always end in 'ko'.

'Happiness' can be translated as 'Sachi', so her name in Japanese would be 'Sachiko'.

'Flower' is 'Hano', so Miss Flower's name would be 'Hanoko', or, with the title 'Miss', 'Hanoko san'.

Star Festival. In Japanese this is called 'Panabapar' and is held in the evening of the seventh day of the seventh month.

As Nona said, it is in memory of two lovers separated on earth. Their spirits are in two stars and on this night they are allowed to meet across the Milky Way.

The wish papers are sold in the shops; they are of soft paper coloured yellow or red or green and are twisted up and hung on the good luck bamboos. Often children just brush the words 'River of Heaven'.

Kneeling. No Japanese girl of good manners would remain standing when there were elders or guests present. She would also kneel to serve tea or food.

The cushions are flat, stuffed with wadded cotton, almost like little eiderdowns.

Haiku. The haiku is a tiny verse form in which Japanese poets have been working for hundreds of years. They have only seventeen syllables (a syllable is a word or part of a word that makes one sound: for instance, 'shut' is one syllable, 'sha-dow' is two); as you can imagine they are very difficult to write and to translate.

As Miss Lane said, there are different haiku for different times of year (though on the scrolls a proverb or a single word is often used instead of a poem). In case you want to make up haiku or use them on scrolls, I give four different ones for Spring, Summer, Autumn and Winter:

Spring: My two plum trees are
So gracious . . .
See, they flower
One now, one later.

Summer: What a peony . . .
Demanding to be
Measured
By my little fan!

Autumn: Cruel autumn wind
Cutting to the
Very bones . . .
Of my poor scarecrow.

Winter: Three loveliest things
Moonlight . . . cherry-
Bloom . . . Now I go
To see silent snow.

But you may like to make up your own.

Firebox. Each Japanese room has one of these, called a hibachi. They are lacquered wood outside, earthenware lined, and they glow with a few pieces of charcoal in a bed of ashes. The doors slide open and you can warm your hands or boil a kettle for tea or rice. Very often in real houses the fireboxes are sunk in the floor.

Flower Arranging. Japanese girls of good family spend some months in learning how to arrange flowers, for Japanese flower arrangement – Ikebana – is an art.

In one side of every room is the tokonoma or niche. It is a place of honour as the fireplace is in Western homes. Its floor is raised higher than the rest of the room and it is here that the flowers are placed, only one or two, with twigs and leaves arranged in a pattern . . . and every flower or branch has its meaning.

The Lamp. The house lamp was made from a cotton reel. Tom stained the empty reel dark brown to make the stand, then ran a flex up through the hole in the reel; a small size bulb fitted into the top, and Nona made a shade of tracing paper and joined it into a circle with sticky-tape. Tom cut a groove round the top of the cotton reel on which it could stand, and the lamp was done.

A selected list of titles available from Macmillan Children's Books

The prices shown below are correct at the time of going to press. However, Macmillan Publishers reserves the right to show new retail prices on covers, which may differ from those previously advertised.

Rumer Godden

The Fairy Doll	ISBN-13: 978-0-330-44226-8	£9.99
	ISBN-10: 0-330-44226-0	
The Story of Holly and Ivy	ISBN-13: 978-0-330-43974-9	£4.99
	ISBN-10: 0-330-43974-X	
The Dolls' House	ISBN-13: 978-0-330-44255-8	£4.99
	ISBN-10: 0-330-44255-4	

For older readers

The Peacock Spring	ISBN-13: 978-0-330-39738-4	£5.99
	ISBN-10: 0-330-39738-9	
The Greengage Summer	ISBN-13: 978-0-330-39737-7	£5.99
	ISBN-10: 0-330-39737-0	

All Pan Macmillan titles can be ordered from our website, www.panmacmillan.com, or from your local bookshop and are also available by post from:

Bookpost, PO Box 29, Douglas, Isle of Man IM99 1BQ
Credit cards accepted. For details:
Telephone: 01624 677237
Fax: 01624 670923
Email: bookshop@enterprise.net
www.bookpost.co.uk

Free postage and packing in the United Kingdom